# The Secret of the POOJA Bears

## Angel Voices & Candlelight

**Aideen McGinley**

Balboa Press books may be ordered through booksellers or by contacting:

Balboa Press
A Division of Hay House
1663 Liberty Drive
Bloomington, IN 47403
www.balboapress.com
1 (877) 407-4847

ISBN: 978-1-5043-9078-1 (sc)
ISBN: 978-1-5043-9079-8 (e)

Library of Congress Control Number: 2017916529

Print information available on the last page.

Balboa Press rev. date: 11/13/2017

BALBOA.
PRESS
A DIVISION OF HAY HOUSE

# Hope And Hugs

The **POOJA** Bears are named after a special little girl who lives in Bawana, a resettlement colony in New Delhi. **POOJA** is the Sanskrit for prayer.

Help **POOJA** Bears spread hope and hugs. Help support children and families across the world by buying this book and a bear for those who matter to you most, young and old!

All proceeds from this book and the **POOJA** Bears will go to two very special charities.

# The Charities

The Aisling Centre promotes positive mental health and emotional well-being. Adults and children come to the Centre at difficult times in their lives, many in distress and despair. At the Centre they can find hope and healing in a welcoming, safe and supportive environment.
For more information, go to www.theaislingcentre.com

Habitat for Humanity works where it matters most -at the heart of communities. Every day, in Northern Ireland and 70 countries, it partners with families to build or improve their home; a safe place for children to learn and families to thrive.

Get involved today: habitatni.co.uk/poojabear

## The Story Begins...

The **POOJA** Bears live in a very special place. They live in St Michael's Church Enniskillen since 1875. The beautiful church has one of the highest roofs in Ireland and is the perfect place to live and play in their secret hideout.

The **POOJA** Bears feel very honoured to live in a wonderful place. From here they watch life in all its guises. Happy people, sad people. People looking for hope, health and healing. Their secret is that not everyone can see them. Can you?

They have a very special hug that helps everyone to cope, be happy and see life in a more positive light.

Come and meet the **POOJA** Bears ...

# Angel Voices

St Michael's have a wonderful organ with 1818 pipes which create a heavenly sound.

Pippa **POOJA** Bear was always singing. She just loved to sing in the choir.

But one day out of the blue
Pippa **POOJA** Bear lost her voice.
She was scared and sad.
All the **POOJA** Bears and her friends in the choir
searched the church high and low.
All day long.
But as night fell
it was nowhere to be found.
Her friends told her not to give up hope.

Her friends had to go home.
The **POOJA** Bears fell exhausted into their beds.
But Pippa **POOJA** Bear couldn't sleep.

She was so sad.

Would she ever be able to sing again?
As dawn broke she fell into a deep sleep
and dreamt of the joy of singing with the angels.
When she woke she felt something warm
and soft around her neck.
It was a beautiful butterfly scarf.

She smiled and knew that everything would be well.
She slowly opened her mouth
And out came the most beautiful notes.
They echoed around the church.
The **POOJA** Bears woke to the wonderful sound
They smiled and cheered to hear her sing again.

She never found out who gave her the scarf
but from that day on Pippa **POOJA** Bear never took it off.
She gave joy to all who heard her
With her voice of an angel that was heaven sent.

PAWS
FOR
THOUGHT...

# Never give up hope

# Candlelight

Peter **POOJA** Bear always wanted to be a fireman.
His favourite place in the whole world
was beside the candles.
Every day he watched people lighting them.

Some were happy. Some were sad.
He watched the candles flicker and glow
holding people's dreams and wishes.

Then one day
he heard Joseph and Bruce outside
playing football before coming into the church.

Joseph left his water bottle behind on the seat.
Peter POOJA Bear could not believe his luck.
His eyes lit up.

He skipped back to the candles with the water bottle and with one "**swoosh**" the candles all went out!
What fun!

Day after day Jimmy the caretaker was puzzled.
No matter how often he lit and relit the candles they went out.
Peter **POOJA** Bear giggled in the background.

One day Aideen and Evie came into the church.
They were really sad.
They were lighting a special candle
for their great grandad Joe, but it was always going out!!!

They started to cry.
Their tears fell onto Peter POOJA Bear's head.
He felt really bad.

Peter **POOJA** Bear leapt up
and gave them both
the biggest hug he could.
They hugged him back
and he promised never
to put out the candles ever again.

PAWS
FOR
THOUGHT...

Always think
how your actions
affect others.

# The POOJA Bears Hugging Game

A hug from a **POOJA** Bear is a very special thing. The bears help play the hugging game at the end of the day.
Bedtime is a special time to talk about the day that has been and what is to come tomorrow.
The word **BEAR** has a special meaning.
**POOJA** Bears use their PAWS to spell.

**B** Is **BE** grateful for one thing today.

**E** Share the things that **EXCITED** you today.

**A** Highlight an **ACHIEVEMENT** you made today.

**R** **REFLECT** and look forward to tomorrow.

# The Gift That Keeps On Giving...

To join us in our giving and support the vital work of our two charities go to habitatni.co.uk/poojabear

# About The Author...

©Habitat for Humanity

This book was inspired by my children, my grandchildren and other children I have had the privilege to meet in Ireland, India, Thailand, Chile.

Thanks to Sheila, Michael, Sandra, Bridie, Jenny, Jimmy, Monsignor Peter, Connor, Pat and ALL my family and friends for believing in the **POOJA** Bears.

*Aideen*

Lightning Source UK Ltd.
Milton Keynes UK
UKOW07f0240301117
313562UK00006B/121/P

9 781504 390781